Catholic Tales for Boys and Girls

Catholic Tales for Boys and Girls

by Caryll Houselander

Illustrated by Renée George

SOPHIA INSTITUTE PRESS®
Manchester, New Hampshire

The stories in *Catholic Tales for Boys and Girls* were originally published in *The Children's Messenger*, London, and were published by Sheed and Ward in 1957 in a single volume entitled *Terrible Farmer Timson and Other Stories*.

Printed in the United States of America

Cover design by Theodore Schluenderfritz

Sophia Institute Press®
Box 5284, Manchester, NH 03108
1-800-888-9344
www.sophiainstitute.com

Library of Congress Cataloging-in-Publication Data

Houselander, Caryll.
Catholic tales for boys and girls / Caryll Houselander ; illustrated by Renée George.
p. cm.
Previously published under title: Terrible Farmer Timson and other stories. New York : Sheed and Ward, 1957.
ISBN 1-928832-74-1 (alk. paper)
1. Children's stories, English. 2. Christian life — Juvenile fiction. [1. Christian life—Fiction. 2. Short stories.] I. George, Renée, ill. II. Title.
PZ7.H8165 Cat 2002
[Fic] — dc2 2002015880

Contents

Catholic Tales for Boys and Girls

Terrible Farmer Timson

Jill and Audrey woke up in the farmhouse bedroom on the first morning of the summer holidays. At first they were not awake enough to know just why they felt so happy. Then the sounds and smells of the holidays gathered into the morning: the cock crowing (a scarlet sound like a pennon blown out curling on the wind), the sound of milk cans and hobnailed boots on flagstones, the sound of voices that were slow and burred and spoke words that were brown and velvet like the bees' backs, the smell of grass in the early sun and of clover in the grass.

All day their delight folded and took new shapes: getting the eggs for breakfast and feeling them warm and softly polished in the palm of one's hand, wearing old blue overalls and no shoes or stockings or gloves or hats, picking fruit and eating it outdoors, and at last evening, and night bringing a darkness that was gentle and moved along under the trees in the orchard like deep blue clouds, and stars among the branches like golden fruit.

Jill and Audrey remembered that all the loveliness of the day was God's gift, and then they remembered the promise they had made: that although they were alone, in the charge of Mrs. Brown, who was not a Catholic, they would ask George Brown to drive them to Mass in the pony cart every Sunday. For tomorrow was Sunday.

George, however, shook his head; the pony had gone lame. Jill said, "It doesn't matter. We could walk." But Mrs. Brown laughed at the very idea. "It's four miles there and four miles back," she said. "That's eight miles. You couldn't walk eight miles, and what's more, Almighty God would not expect it of you."

Audrey said slowly, "No, perhaps He wouldn't, and anyway it wouldn't be a sin not to go; but really, we *do* walk eight miles in the fields, I'm sure, and if God doesn't expect it, it would make Him all the happier, like giving Him a surprise."

"Course," said George, "if you be that set on going, it is a shortcut through Farmer Timson's land — only, if he caught you, he'd carry on terrible: he don't let no one cross his land; a fair caution he is!"

"Couldn't we ask him?"

"Well, you *could*, but there's no saying what he'd say."

"Well, we'll try," said Audrey, and taking the candle from the kitchen table and holding it above her like a star, she climbed the wooden stairs to the bedroom.

Farmer Timson had had a miserable day. Saturday was always a black day with him. He sat in his little lovely wood and stared through the big leaves, and just because the leaves were all lovely with the light of the evening, he was all the more wretched. He picked a wildflower and crushed it between his big finger and thumb; it hurt him to see it looking so frail and lovely when he felt himself to be so rotten. Yes, rotten, that's what he felt!

When he was a boy, and even when he was a man, Saturday was Confession day, and he had looked forward to it — yes, looked forward to coming back along the white road into this very wood and feeling that now that he was free of all his sins, the flowers and the birds and all the lovely wild things were his friends.

Then the foolish man had quarreled with the priest, a priest who had been dead many years now, and so he had not gone to the church along the road anymore. And he had put notices up all around his fences, forbidding people to pass. And everyone had forgotten that old Timson had ever been a Catholic — everyone but he. He was a fair caution now, as George said, a man with his heart aching for something he couldn't have, just because his own silly self would not let him be humble enough to go and get it. But he was so unhappy that he simply had to pretend to himself that he was very fierce and terrible and didn't mind a bit. When people came to ask him timidly if they might take the shortcut through his land, he shouted, "No!" so angrily that in the end no one came anymore.

On this particular Saturday, he was lonelier than ever, so he crushed flowers in his fingers and tried to think of some notice to put up that would be even more alarming than the others. Sitting contentedly in the grass and the white clover, a red cow gazed at him with her quiet eyes. She sat in a field just beyond the wood; so still she was that she might have been one of those cardboard cows that gaze so gently across the manger in the crib at Christmastime.

"Idiot," said Farmer Timson, looking at her. "Idiot!" And when in return for this unprovoked insult, she gazed at him all the more softly, lying quite still, he went into the toolshed and prepared a new notice: "Beware of the Mad Bull!"

Audrey and Jill stood a little doubtfully outside Farmer Timson's gate. It was useless to deny that their Sunday clothes lessened their courage. And when they discovered that they could pass through Farmer Timson's land only at the cost of persecution, their hearts sank. For there in front of them was the notice: "Trespassers will be Persecuted." That is what it seemed to say, but the letters were a little worn with weather and age. Audrey's eyes grew big.

"You've often said," remarked Jill, "that you would like to be persecuted."

"Ye-es," said Audrey doubtfully, "I did use to think perhaps I'd like to be a martyr. I'm sure I would *after* I'd been eaten by the lion, only I've never thought of how it would be *before*."

"Sometimes the lions turn out to be tame, like Daniel's."

"Yes, but not *always*."

"Well, we'd better go on."

They went on to the gate and there across the top bars they read, "Beware: Savage Dogs."

"Oh! That's worse than lions!" said Audrey.

"No, it isn't. Dogs don't eat you."

"No, but they bite; and then instead of being a martyr who's forgotten he was ever eaten, you're a bitten person who's not in Heaven."

Jill felt she must stop Audrey from talking. "When you aren't worthy to be eaten," she said, "God might be pleased to allow you to be only bitten."

And very firmly she opened the gate. Just then a dog came slowly out of the bushes wagging its tail, a fat, white, smiling dog. "Look," said Jill. "God *is* making the dogs tame. We'd better have more faith. Come on."

So with the dog trotting beside them, they crossed the first field and came into the small wood. It was very still and filled only with the sound of bird notes and bird wings and the crackling of the twigs where they walked. Their white kid shoes became green with moss, and once or twice their dresses were torn on thorns. As to their gloves, they became filthy, but otherwise they went safely and began to feel quite brave again about martyrdom. But they were unaware that Farmer Timson himself was hidden among the trees at the far edge of the wood.

"You see," said Jill, patting the dog's head, "it's all right after all; there aren't any savage dogs or lions."

"Well, I think," Audrey answered, "that God softened the dog's heart for our sakes, so it may be He'll soften the farmer's, too."

"Well, George said he is a fair caution."

"Yes, but a fair caution isn't awfuller than a savage dog. Poor old man. I feel sorry for him, being so angry when all the things around him are so gentle."

Farmer Timson, hiding in the trees, scowled. "So I'm being run down behind my back," he thought to himself. But he waited, and suddenly Jill and Audrey stood stock still and gasped.

Audrey spoke first, in a very small voice. "Jill," she said, "do you see? 'Beware of the *Mad Bull!*' "

Jill nodded. Her throat had gone dry. As a matter of fact, she was a *little* afraid even of cows when George Brown wasn't there. "What shall we do?"

This time Audrey was braver. "Let's pray to God to turn the bull sensible and gentle, and then go on."

"But suppose God doesn't!"

"Then —" said Audrey suddenly, drawing a deep breath and holding it in, "let's go on and offer it up for Farmer Timson to be turned gentle and sensible."

"We-ell," said Jill, doing the same kind of breath, "I suppose we'd better."

Farmer Timson leaned forward among the leaves. Until now, these two children had been just voices to him. Now, very softly, he parted leaves with his big fingers and peeped at them. What he saw was two small girls who looked smaller still to him because he was a big man.

Jill and Audrey held hands tightly and stepped into the field, just like the martyrs used to step into the Colosseum at Rome. Little girls were an unusual sight in this field, and the red cow was an inquisitive old animal. She twitched a fly from her ear, whisked her tail, and prepared to stand up. Audrey and Jill began to run.

Farmer Timson, who was suddenly overcome with shame at his own mean trick, ran too, out of the green wood, after them. One glance over their shoulder showed a more awful sight than even a standing-up bull. It showed a huge, red-faced man, who could be no other than the terrible farmer, in full chase. Jill and Audrey ran the faster. Behind them a voice thundered, "There are *no* savage dogs; there are *no* mad bulls!" But "Savage dogs, mad bulls" was all that they heard.

They ran on, stumbling on the tufts of grass. Their hats blew off, and they never thought of picking them up. Farmer Timson yelled again, "There are only kind dogs, gentle cows." But still they ran. Then quite close they heard again, "*Kind* dogs, *gentle* cows," and a huge hand seized each child by the shoulder.

Ten minutes later, Audrey and Jill, their hats held carefully for them by Farmer Timson, were washing their faces under the tap in Farmer Timson's scullery. Then he prepared two mugs of milk. Certainly God had heard their prayer, for a more gentle and sensible old man they had never met.

"You sit down," he said, "and drink your milk while I get out the pony trap. I'll drive you to Mass, and you'll be there in fine time."

"I don't think we're fit to go into church now," said Audrey.

"It's *I* who am not fit to go," said the farmer. "Would you believe it? I've let my soul get all muddied up like your dresses and shoes, just because I was too big a coward to say I was sorry to God. But there's time to put that right before Mass, too. So come along."

"You, a coward?" said Jill. "I thought you were a caution!"

"Aye, and maybe I was that, too; but when I saw you little scraps going past what you thought was a mad bull because you wanted to help me, I just gave up being a coward and a caution, too. So hurry up now, for the priest is busy on a Sunday and I've got to make my confession before Mass."

The Embroidered Coat

Long ago some Japanese nuns took in washing and orphans, the washing to get money to feed and clothe the orphans. When they were tiny, the orphans slept in round baskets filled with cushions. When they grew older, they learned to pray, to sew, to play on little reed pipes, and to enjoy being alive.

One of these orphans, named Mimosa Mary, thought that never was anyone on earth happier than she was. Everything reminded her of the Child Jesus. When the nuns made the white soap flakes foam up in the washing tubs, she thought of the lambs, whiter than snow, that He loves. When the new orphans were brought in and put into the baskets, she thought of the newborn God in His crib.

Opposite the convent was a palace behind high walls. From the convent garden, you could see only the golden dome. The garden behind the high walls was a paradise. It was full of delicate bridges arched over shining streams. So exquisite were the flowers that each was like a carved jewel, and the birds singing in the trees sang with voices like starlight.

Inside the palace, it was as lovely as outside, and here, bowed to all day long by many servants, lived a princess. She, also, was an orphan. She was just the same age as Mimosa. Her name was Lotus Flower.

When Lotus Flower got up in the morning, a line of twenty servants stood by her bed, and her garments were passed from hand to hand until, finally, the chief lady-in-waiting put them on her. After this wearisome event, Lotus Flower went to her lessons. All the tutors bowed to the earth before asking her questions, but all the same, they scolded her severely if she did not know the answers. After lessons came lunch, which again was handed to her, dish after silver dish, through twenty pairs of hands.

And so the day went on until night came and the princess lay in her high bed, her dark slanting eyes fixed on the big, golden star that looked in at the window and said, "Good night."

"Good night," said the golden star, "poor little princess, good night. There is no one to love you. Good night." (But to Mimosa, in her narrow, white bed in the dormitory, the star said, "Good night, Mimosa. God loves you. Good night.")

In Japan people wear embroidered coats, and very often the embroidery tells a story in pictures. Lovers have such coats made for their dear ones, and mothers for their children. But for Lotus Flower, there was no one to think of a message to embroider. She was magnificent but alone.

Nevertheless, since she had to have richer and more splendid coats than anyone else, her ministers sought for people to embroider them. They asked for no picture, however, only for flowers and birds, but they said that the workmanship must be very good. As the nuns were so nearby and were known to be good at sewing, it was only natural that one day the servants of the princess sent across a little coat to be embroidered by them.

Mimosa was in the room, painting a picture on rice paper, with a brush made from a duck's feather, when the royal servant arrived. He was shy, because he was not a Christian and knew no nuns. He explained why he had come and showed a beautiful shining coat of dusk-blue silk.

"What design," said Sister Spirit-of-Light, "would you like? What message or poem to be told for the princess?"

"Oh, none!" the servant said and smiled sadly. "You know, there is no one to think of designs of that sort. Put some flowers and birds on it." When he had bowed himself out, Mimosa came and stood by Sister Spirit-of-Light. She put her small golden hand on the nun's knee and looked into her face. "Does that mean," she said, "that no one loves the princess?"

"Poor little girl," said the nun. "She is an orphan. She is very grand and has no one to play with."

"But *we* are orphans, and we have people to play with! Could she not play with us?"

"Ah, Mimosa, you are not really orphans, for our Lord and His Mother have adopted you. But you are not grand enough to play with Princess Lotus Flower; no one in the land is grand enough."

Mimosa frowned a little, thinking. Her oval face, palely gold and clear, looked like a flower going to sleep. "May I embroider the coat?" she said.

"You! But first of all, you do not like to sit still sewing for long at a time, and second, I am afraid you are not very good at it!"

"Sister, I will be very patient. I will try very hard."

The sister looked well at her. Then she said, "Very well. You may try."

The threads were brought, scarlet and green and white and gold and many other colors, and Mimosa set to work. Every time before she began, she washed her hands very clean and said a prayer. Then she sat under the flowering trees and began to embroider the story she wanted to tell the princess.

Over the place where the princess's heart would be, Mimosa did the Infant Jesus in His round cradle-basket, and she sewed His Heart in threads of gold. Above, at the neck, she made a star, "our star" she called it, but it was meant also for the Star of Bethlehem. The hands of our Lord were held out, and our Lady, who sat by Him, was beckoning; she beckoned toward a tiny picture of the castle wall, with the trees just showing over the top; and all around the hem, beckoning too, the orphans danced.

"Well, it is a little clumsy," said Sister Spirit-of-Light, "and the picture is unusual. That hem part might even be thought a little impudent if its message is really understood, but people hardly ever look carefully enough at pictures on coats to understand. And I know, Mimosa, that every stitch was a prayer."

When Mimosa said good night to the star that night, "Oh, let her understand!" she whispered.

And Lotus Flower *did* understand. The very next day, she was outside the convent gates, peering in, and it was Mimosa herself who drew back the lock.

When the princess was found to be missing, a hue and cry arose. Not only did the Grand Vizier himself set out to look for her, but all the warriors, too, armed and on horseback. They wore silver armor with blue and red tassels, and their horses were like white Shetland ponies, with trappings of scarlet and silver horns fastened between their eyes.

And while these warriors waited in the courtyard for the word of command, a beggar, who had just come from the convent, where he had had a meal, told the captain that he was certain the princess was in there among the orphans. This news made the captain and the Grand Vizier furious.

"What!" they cried, "with those children who have not one drop of royal blue blood in their veins! If it is so, we will certainly have all their heads cut off. And," they added as an afterthought, "all the nuns' heads, too."

And over they went with a great blowing of trumpets and clattering of hoofs to the convent gates.

The orphans were very excited to see this army of warriors at their gates, and ran to stare. And there, sure enough, in their midst, her hair untidy, her eyes shining, her face flushed, wearing her new dress, was the princess.

The captain's face blazed bright red. He was about to seize his royal mistress and to begin cutting off heads, when someone who had been hidden among the other children separated himself from them and came to meet him.

It was a Boy whom all could see was a King. He wore a robe on which the sun and the moon were embroidered and on His head a crown.

The captain sprang from his horse and fell on one knee, and all the others bowed low. "I did not know," said the captain, "that here was a great King."

That is how it happened that the princess went every day to play with the orphans, and she and all her court learned to pay homage to the King of Kings.

The Curé's Guest

Monsieur le Curé is coming!" old Hortense said, looking out of her doorway to the middle of the village street.

She said this, not because she could see him in the distance, but because Marie Angèle had begun to dance in the road in her most brazen way, and Jean to beat loudly on his tin drum. All the other children were clapping and shouting to them to go on.

But Monsieur le Curé only smiled as he passed and spoke a word of greeting. After that he read his breviary and seemed not to notice the long legs and frantic gestures of Marie Angèle and Jean, and the clapping of the others.

It was a very sad village. It had hardly one good Catholic in it. It used to have a Catholic school, but this had failed because the people would not support it. Now there was only the government school, where the schoolmaster taught the children to laugh at their priest, and the children thought they were great and fine to do it.

Marie Angèle did not really like leaping and capering in the blazing sun; Jean did not like beating his drum for her leaping. They did it because each of them thought the other would think it bold and clever. Monsieur le Curé smiled and passed. Even old Hortense felt inclined to cuff the two children for their impudence and stupidity and for leading all the others into it; but she and many of the grownups in their village had learned the same folly in the same school.

Monsieur le Curé was very poor. He lived in a little cottage on the hill that he swept and cleaned himself, and he cooked his own meals. Although he was very humble, he used to draw the blinds when he cooked, because some of the children stared in at the window and made fun of him. He mended his own clothes, too, because there was no one else to do it, and he was a very tidy man.

Sometimes an old man or woman fell ill, and the curé would come to see them; then they often shouted at him to go away. And when he had gone, they would be afraid of death and send for him to return, and he would come back, even late at night in the rain, because he loved them all and felt sorry for them.

Every Sunday, after the curé had read the notices at Mass, he used to say, "The children will all be welcome to tea at the rectory this afternoon." The children never went, not even one. But nonetheless, every Saturday night, the curé went to the baker's shop and bought a big bag of penny buns: not dull buns that are the same all around, but those made like little bald men with currants for eyes, or like little women with umbrellas made out of gingerbread. And everyone, especially Marie Angèle and Jean, longed to eat the buns at the curé's cottage; but they wouldn't, for fear the others would say they had been conquered with a gingerbread lady or a bun-man.

Poor Marie Angèle was an especially greedy little girl, and she had no pennies. Sometimes she peeped into the candy store on a Saturday and saw Monsieur le Curé buying a large bag of brightly colored candies. They were her favorite sort, and sometimes when she was in bed on Saturday night, she could not help thinking of candy until her mouth watered, and she wished the next old lady who got frightened of dying would send *her* to fetch the curé.

One very hot, shining Sunday, Marie Angèle and Jean were sitting at the side of the hedge. At the top of the hill they could see the curé's cottage.

"It's a funny thing," said Jean, "that he goes on buying candy and buns and no one eats them."

"Yes," said Marie Angèle, "and it's a funny thing that he never seems to mind. I mean, he always speaks to us."

"Yes, and smiles," said Jean.

"I would like to know what he does with the buns and candy," said Marie Angèle.

"I suppose he guzzles them all himself," said Jean.

"It would be rather fun," said Marie Angèle slowly, looking at Jean out of the corner of her eye, "to go and peep in at the window. Then we'd know."

"Yes," said Jean doubtfully, "but he'd see us, and he might drag us in to preach at us. That's all he wants really: to make us learn catechism."

Marie Angèle sighed. "We can't be *sure* he would. Anyhow, we could say we *wouldn't* learn."

"I'm not going. I believe *you* like him," said Jean, who liked the curé himself and longed to go.

"There is no one to see us if we do go," said Marie Angèle.

"Yes, there is," Jean answered suddenly. "There is someone coming up the hill, a boy."

Marie Angèle peeped over the hedge. "So there is! I've never seen him before. Have you?"

Jean stared. "No. Look, do you see how the sun moves along behind his head? It is so dazzling, you can't see his face."

"And see," said Marie Angèle, "he has fallen and hurt himself; his hands are bleeding!"

"And his feet," said Jean. "He must have come on the stony road and fallen on it."

"No, I think he has fallen in the thorn bush. Don't you see? There are thorns caught in his hair. I wonder why he doesn't pull them out."

"Let's watch where he goes," said Jean.

They crouched behind the hedge, and the boy passed them and went on toward the curé's cottage.

"I say," said Marie Angèle, "I do *really* want to follow him."

"You want the candy," said Jean sulkily. His own feet were dancing to follow, and he was angry because he didn't know why. But the boy had disappeared into the cottage, and Marie Angèle was already running up the hill, so Jean ran after her.

When they got to the cottage, they crept to the window and looked in. They saw a most unexpected thing. The boy was dancing — not like Marie Angèle, but a gentle little child's dance. The curé was beating an old drum like Jean's, only laughing and not with a set, angry face.

And as they watched, something very strange happened. First the boy seemed to be Marie Angèle herself while he danced, only the little flashing feet were bare and bleeding. And then he turned into Jean and took the drum and beat it, only the hands that clasped the drumsticks were torn. And after that, he seemed to be a lot of children they knew, and these children all sat around the curé and ate his buns and candy and talked to him.

And presently the curé told them about Jesus Christ, who dwells in children's hearts and is the kindness and goodness in them; and how the children comforted him, the curé, and made up for the grownups; and how they must be as sweet and gentle to them as to himself, and teach them about the little Lord.

As they listened, the two children saw that, after all, only one Boy was there, sitting on the stool at the priest's feet, smiling tenderly at him. The sun was still behind His head, the thorns still in His hair . . . and at last they understood.

For a long time, they stood, hanging their heads. Then Marie Angèle whispered, "It is the Christ Child pretending to be us, so that the curé won't know we haven't come."

"Then," whispered Jean, "He must be pretending to be something very mean and horrid."

"No," said Marie Angèle. "He is pretending to be us, as we would be if we let Monsieur le Curé give Him to us; then He would live in our souls and make us nice."

Jean was silent then. He said, "We are very proud, and God is very humble then."

"Yes," said Marie Angèle.

On the next Sunday, and all the Sundays after it, the whole company of children in the village went up the hill to the cottage, and two of them knew that a little Boy with wounded feet led them. Now when Monsieur le Curé passes through the village, Marie Angèle still dances and Jean beats his drum, but it is a pretty and pleasant dance, and the drummer laughs and smiles at the audience. Yet it is the same dance

and the same music that the curé had always seen and heard, because he had always seen the children as if they were as generous and beautiful as God meant them to be.

If I Were You

Louis came softly into the church at the end of a day's work in the fields. It had been a bad day. When they were bringing in the harvest, the rain had come down, and whenever the rain came now, it made Father angry. "We shall be ruined by the rain," he would say. When Father was angry, they were all sad, boys and girls working side by side in the fields. It was like a gray cloud covering the blue sky; they began to think of being grown up and having to earn their bread. The rain had soaked Louis's clothes, and he was wet and cold. It had been a long day: rising before dark to feed the pigs, helping Mother in the kitchen, and then the fields and the rain!

He looked at the statue of the Child Jesus, the oval face of pale wood, the faint smile, and the wide, sightless eyes. He looked at the large crown and the vestment heavy with gold and the golden shoes. "If I were You, Jesus," he said, "I would make everyone happy. I would make them rich, I would make the sun to shine on the harvest fields, and I would convert the whole world."

The small, pale head of the statue turned slowly, and the eyes fixed gravely upon Louis. "But that," He said, "is your work, Louis!"

"My work?"

"Yes. Do I not live in your heart? Am I not the treasure and richness of the world? Am I not the sun that never sets?"

"Why, yes," said Louis, twisting the front of his blue smock in his hands, "certainly, as the curé says, it is so. You live in my heart, because I am baptized and in grace. But I cannot show that. I am very poor; You have Your crown that shows You are king and Your gold vestment that shows

You are high priest, and Your glory around You to show You are God. If You would just come down and walk through our fields and into our houses, everyone would see how great and how rich You are. Then they would trust You and love You, and they would not be out of temper when it rains on the crops."

"I will lend you my crown and my vestment and my glory, and you shall walk in your own fields in my golden shoes," said the Child Jesus. And as He spoke, He undid the great clasp of His vestment, and lifting His crown, He held it out to Louis.

With trembling hands, Louis drew his smock over his head and took off his wooden shoes, and he vested himself and put on the crown and the shoes of gold, while the statue of the holy Child took the peasant's clothes and put them on Himself.

"I feel afraid," said Louis. "They will know me by my face, and what will happen when they see my old faded smock on You?"

"No," said the statue, "for I have also lent you my glory, and in its light, your face, too, will seem to be mine. Now I give you all my riches. Go and convert the world."

"I will," Louis answered. "At least I will convert our own hamlet, which is the same thing. But, dear Jesus, You look a little funny in my poor clothes!"

"No funnier than I always look in you, Louis." And Jesus picked up the round world, which He had put down while He changed His clothes, and turned His head as it had been before, and was still again and silent.

Louis went slowly over the fields. His shoes glittered on the sodden stubble. He saw that the wounds on his hands shone like jewels. When he came to the pond near his father's farm, he looked into it. It was a green, dark pond, but as he looked down, he saw that the light of his glory had changed it to a mirror of silver, and in the silver, among the crimson clouds of the dusk, he saw the radiance of the Christ Child's face.

"First," he said softly, "I will convert the richest man I know, and he will pay all of us highly for our produce, and give new shoes to the curé and a monstrance of solid gold to the church!"

Usually he approached the big house timidly, by the back door, but now he walked up the drive, his head held high, his eyes aflame with joy, and he rang the bell loudly. No sooner had the butler opened the door than he gave a cry of terror and slammed it shut. He ran panic-stricken to his master.

"Sir," he cried, "there is our Lord at the door, crowned and ablaze with glory!"

At first the rich man refused to believe this, but at last he looked out the window and saw the child below, lifting his hands, imploring him to open the door. The poor man sank back on the sofa and covered his face with his hands. "He has come to take me to the throne of judgment," he groaned.

The butler cleared his throat. "I regret it, sir, deeply," he said politely, "and I may say, I am sure, that you will be deeply lamented by the whole staff. At the same time, sir, may I venture to suggest that you have led a good, indeed an exemplary, life!"

"Don't be a fool," wailed the rich man. "You know perfectly well that mine isn't the figure to squeeze through the eye of a needle; any camel could do it more easily. I always thought I'd be able to get rid of some of my riches before the end — right at the last, you know, when I'd be too ill to enjoy them. I never thought He would come for me suddenly!"

"Perhaps, sir, He would consent to wait, while you give your property to the poor."

There was another loud peal on the bell.

"Yes, yes. Ask Him to wait, outside."

The butler coughed. "Sir, under the circumstances, it might be discreet to approach the Almighty yourself!"

Louis was feeling cold. His shoes were pinching him, and he was tired of standing on the doorstep. Suddenly an upstairs window was flung open, and the stricken face of the rich man appeared. "Please, please," he called hoarsely, "will you go away? I am not ready for you. I am afraid!" Louis turned away.

"Shall I start packing things up, sir?" said the butler.

"No, He has gone. I'm not going tonight, after all."

"I mean, sir, packing things up to give away."

"Tomorrow, tomorrow," said the rich man as he gazed, fearfully, out the window.

But the little figure of Louis was far away. The glory surrounding him looked only like a lantern swung in a man's hand through the darkness. "I will go to our neighbor, who is a farmer like us," said Louis. "For although he is already good, he is like my father, sad and angry when the weather is against the harvest; he does not trust very much in God when it rains."

Through the open windows of the farmhouse came the murmur of low voices speaking together. The family were kneeling for their night prayers.

"O God," said the farmer, "bless our crops, and deign to dwell in our hearts."

"Deign to dwell in our hearts," said the children after him, and in the candlelight, their faces were downy like flowers dusted with pollen.

Louis tapped on the window ledge. Startled, the family sprang to their feet, and seeing the blaze of the gold and the jewels in the fire of glory and the great crown on the child's head, they shrank back against the whitewashed wall of the kitchen. Their eyes were huge and black in their faces. They huddled against their own long shadows, like sheep crowding together in a storm.

"Let me come in," said Louis.

But the farmer threw himself on his knees again, and clasping his hands cried, "No, no, Lord. Our house is too poor, too mean and dirty. We are only ordinary people. Do not ask me to let You come in!"

"But you asked me to come!"

"O Lord, we prayed only that You would dwell in our hearts invisibly, not in our wretched home in Your glory! Look at the rickety chairs, the hard beds, the uneven flagstones. We have too little to give You. I beg You to let us remain as we are and to leave us!" And because he could not bear to see the poor man so upset, Louis turned away.

"There is the very holy man who lives alone and prays all day," he thought. "I will go to him, for now it is getting so late, and I am tired and hungry. If I cannot convert and bless anyone, I can at least eat and rest myself, and I can take off this crown that is making my head ache and these shoes that hurt my feet."

But when the holy man saw the child at his door, he gave a loud cry: "O Lord, depart from me, for I am a sinful man!"

"But I only want to rest a little in your house," said Louis.

"No, no, the house of my spirit is unclean! Have mercy upon me! Do not torment me with Your glory!"

Now Louis began to cry. His hair was tangled in the crown; the vestment was growing terribly heavy; the shoes pinched; and the night was around him like a thick dark cloth. He would have taken off all those things and God's glory, too, and gone to his own home, but he did not have his own clothes to put on, and he was afraid that his mother might not know him.

"I will go to the old charwoman who cleans the church," he said, "for she is used to seeing Jesus in His crown." This time he knocked timidly, but when the old woman saw him, she opened her arms and folded him into them. For she had forgotten self. She had scrubbed the floor beside the Blessed Sacrament so often that she had forgotten everything but God's presence. She did not think of whether she was rich or poor, whether she was good or bad. She did not think whether the glory of God would bless or blind her. She opened her arms and folded him to her heart.

In the morning, with the crown and vestment and the shoes folded into a bundle, clothed in a clean smock, Louis went to the church. A little crowd stood around the statue. They did not notice Louis and his bundle; they had eyes only for the change that had taken place: the statue in Louis's clothes. The rich man was there, the holy man and the farmer with his children, Louis's mother and father, the curé, and many others.

"Look," said Louis's mother, "He has put on the same clothes as our own boys. He must have done it to make us love Him as we love our sons!"

The curé said, "He means to show us that He has put on our poor human nature."

"He means to say," said the rich man, "that He is a working boy, asking the rich for good wages and fair treatment."

"He is showing that He is our friend," said the farmer's little girl, "and He wants to join in our play."

And the holy man said, "It means that He does not want to blind us with His glory."

"He is telling us," said the curé, "that He lives in each one of us and we must thank Him by loving each other with all our hearts."

When the people had gone to the fields, rejoicing, Louis asked, "Is the world too wicked, Jesus, to be converted by Your glory in Heaven?"

And Jesus said, "No, Louis, it is too good. It must be converted by my lowliness in you."

Bird on the Wing

Very still the night; no sounds but the water gently lapping the ships in the harbor, and the banjo of some sailor on board, and now and then, clear and sweet, laughter weaving its way into the sound of music and water.

You would have said a mouse could not stir unheard, yet someone did move unheard on bare feet and climb down the worn wooden steps. He slipped noiselessly into the dark water and swam out to the beautiful ship that lay there with her great white sails and tall masts crowding up to the stars. Silently the swimmer hauled himself up the rope and came aboard. He stood dead still, staring at the broad back of the dozing ship's watchman. Then he dropped down into the hold and crouched there, his face buried in his hands, praying to the Mother of God that the loud beating of his heart would not betray him!

It was the orphan boy Anthony, who had picked up a living these last two years working for sailors and fishermen in the harbor. He still remembered the old days in England before the Faithful were persecuted, when he was a tiny boy and it was not against the law to sing to the Infant Jesus at Christmastime and to gather flowers for God's Mother in May. And since then, more than once, he had seen a priest coming in from the sea, dressed gaily like a man of the world, and go riding inland to carry the word of God, which all the armed men in the world cannot destroy. And now and again, rumors had come of these glad gentlemen being taken and put to death.

Those rumors had thrilled Anthony. Somehow, when he heard them, a voice seemed to speak in his heart, inviting him, too, to be an apostle. When he helped the fishermen to haul in the nets and saw the silver fish swarming in the meshes, he would think of those who were fishers of men, and the dream would open in his mind like a flower opening in the light. "I must get to France," he would think. "Somehow I must get there and be made a priest."

Now, he was fourteen, and still he had put by no money. How could he? And it was not safe to ask advice of anyone. But today the chance had come; the beautiful ship had sailed into the harbor, but not to stay. There was something mysterious about her, old Ben the sailor had said, something mighty queer. Before tomorrow, he said, she would be gone. Her name was *Bird on the Wing*, a queer name for a ship.

Then the thought came to Anthony: "She is bound for France; she is carrying those who are to be priests. Tonight she will be gone, and I, I will be aboard her." He would go aboard secretly. No one would stop him, for no one would know, and then he would go to the captain and beg him to let him work his way to France.

It seemed a long time that he waited, crouching down in the hold. At last he heard the seamen moving about overhead, hauling up the anchors and beginning a sea chantey, and he knew that *Bird on the Wing* was waking from her light sleep and moving out to sea. He felt the sweet stir under him and the grace of her swaying movement. He knew that now she was around the bend facing the open sea, that the wind was gathering in her white sails. She was away, away on the sea, driven by a light wind in the darkness! He felt the lovely rhythm of her movement, the movement of the beautiful ship that was wed now to the waves and the wind, which had wakened her from her sleep and given her life.

Anthony got up from his cramped position and stretched his stiff limbs. Then he clambered up on deck. Yes, they were away, and the lights of the harbor were only little sparks in the distance. But suddenly something gripped his heart, and he stood rooted there, staring. A little flag was fluttering up the mast, a black flag bearing a white skull and crossbones. It fluttered up like a dark quiver of cruel laughter: the flag of a pirate ship!

While he stared at it, a great hand had him by the shoulder, a strong hand with fingers that gripped like iron. A lamp was swung into his face, and voices broke around him in loud cries: "A stowaway! A stowaway!"

He was dragged before the captain, who sat on a barrel, chewing a quid of tobacco. He was a great, swarthy man with a jaw like a shark and a red bandanna around his head, and in his ears he wore golden rings as big as a lady's bracelets. By his side stood the mate, nursing a saber in his arms and smiling with a smile as relentless as the edge of its sharp blade.

"Mate," said the captain, "what does we do with stowaways?"

"Well," drawled the mate, "usually we makes 'em walk the plank."

A loud voice in Anthony's soul called upon God's holy Mother to help him. But out of his mouth came only a weak, shaking voice, speaking to the captain. "Sir," he said, "I did not mean to be a stowaway. I thought you were bound for France and that you would let me work my passage there!"

"Bound for France we may be, or we may be bound for Hell; but if we do go to France, we shall go around the world to get there."

"Then, if you will let me," replied Anthony, "I will work my passage around the world to France."

At this, the ship's doctor was called. He pummeled Anthony's arms, banged him in the chest and back, pinched the calves of his legs, and finally he said, "Maybe he could stand it, but more likely it will kill him." They all laughed heartily, but the captain ordered Anthony to be taken below and set to work.

Hard days followed for Anthony: hauling ropes, climbing the rigging, swabbing the decks, cooking in the hold, washing the dishes, waiting on everyone from the crack of dawn until late at night. He was kicked and cuffed and sent sprawling, and his hands were all blisters, and his feet all scorched from the sun blazing on the deck. Sometimes he was so sore-pressed that he wished he could get sick and die. But then he prayed to his Mother, our Lady, Star of the Sea, to help him, and he set his teeth and went on.

Times were not always so bad, for when they found he was no softy, the pirates were not always cruel, or at least not crueler than they could help. And there was entertainment on board. There were, for example, the yarns of old Jake Smith: strange stories of ships that had been haunted and led to their doom by ghostly gulls, or lured by mermaids; stories of sailors who had foolishly listened to sweet music woven among the waves, or looked down at the water when the mermaids were nearby.

And there was the doctor, who was not an unkind man at heart, although he liked to dwell on the arms and legs he had cut off with a rusty saber in Chinese waters. In his lighter moods, he would open his shirt and roll up his sleeves and show the tattooed pictures all over his skin. And sometimes the Chinese cook got out his banjo, and they would start singing, and there are few things in this world sweeter than the sound of many voices singing at sea.

One morning another ship was sighted. She showed up first on the horizon, so small and far away that the purple sails were no bigger than little curled feathers. As she came closer, they saw that she was no less than a proud Spanish galleon, with a figurehead of gold, and gold ornaments embossed on her sides, and bulwarks of red mahogany. Everyone was ordered on deck, the brass cannons turned their round mouths on her, and the men had their sabers in their hands.

She did not bow her proud spirit, that Spanish ship. She did not surrender lightly; it cost her her very life, that cruel battle in the open sea. And cruel it was. Anthony felt *Bird on the Wing* shuddering from end to end as the guns were fired. He saw the Spanish ship through black clouds of smoke that shut out the very blueness of heaven over them, while she plunged in the waters like a living thing in the throes of death. Her captain and all her crew were on deck fighting for her life. They had golden lace on their coats and great ruffles at their cuffs. But one by one they fell, and their blood flowed out, so that when their ship went down at last, it was a crimson sea that closed over the glory of her.

The crew of the *Bird on the Wing* showed no mercy. Their sabers flashing out in circles around their heads, they went aboard the sinking ship and tore the treasure out of her broken heart and brought it away. Not one of them perished, but the Spaniard went down with all hands to the bottom of the sea.

It was a bitter sight, a sadder thing than Anthony had ever set eyes on, that ship with her purple sails all torn and flung out in pitiful royal tatters, going down into a crimson ocean. A terrible sickness took hold of him, and a great shivering and coldness, and he felt the sweat in his hair, cold like ice and stiff. He saw the pirates, stripped to the waist, their bodies glistening and panting, their ribs heaving up and down with the pumping of their lungs. He saw the captain's face all blackened with smoke, and a trickle of red blood running down on the blackness, but his shark's mouth was grinning terribly, and he was exulting.

In the evening, they unpacked the treasure from the Spanish chests. Anthony sat by them, heartsore, but no one thought of him just then, not even to kick him. He bowed his face in his hands and prayed with a bursting heart, "Mary, my Mother, Mother of God, help me."

When he looked up from his prayer, he saw something in the captain's hands that made his breath come quickly. It was a wooden statue, a statue of our Lady. It was old, and the face was the face of a mother, of mothering itself, a plump, warm, smiling face carved in wood that was dark with age and polished by the gentle caresses of many children's hands. The robes were partly in

dark wood, and partly gilded with an intricate pattern of flowers, and the shoes were gold.

"That should be thrown overboard," said Jake Smith, "for there is no luck in a ship with a woman aboard!"

The captain shook his head. "No," he said, "I'll keep it. It will be a fine doll to take home to my little girl in France. God help the man of you who lays hands on it." And he put it up on the shelf in his own cabin to make an end of the argument.

From that day, life aboard *Bird on the Wing* began to change. The morning after the fight would, in the ordinary way, have been terrible, for now that the excitement was over, the pirates began to feel their cuts and bruises, and the pain of them did not sweeten their tempers. But Anthony knew that things were changing. When he brought in the captain's breakfast, he stood for a moment, praying before the statue. He noticed that the hands were large and rather square, like those of someone who works. They were kind, sensible hands. Then it seemed as if our Lady were speaking to him with a silent voice in his own heart, like music that we sometimes sing in our own minds without any sound. "Bind up their wounds," the voice seemed to say. He put down the tray and went to look for some old shirts to tear up, and when he had found them, he came back and suggested binding the captain's cut forehead.

The captain roared with laughter, but the very violence of his laugh made his head ache more, and he did not look displeased. "Go on, then," he said, and Anthony began. He was not used to such work, and he fumbled with the bandages. Then a strange thing happened.

For a moment (only just a moment, so that he could hardly be sure that it was not only his fancy), his rough, blistered hands seemed to disappear, and the capable hands of the Virgin were working deftly instead.

"You aren't so clumsy as I thought you'd be," said the captain, not unkindly, and Anthony thought that the smile on our Lady's face had grown warmer.

Then he went to Jake Smith and bound his arm, which was horribly cut by a saber. At first, Jake refused. "It will hurt," he said, "and how could a lout like you do it properly?" But when he was bandaged, he looked at Anthony with surprise, and said, "Thank you," a word seldom, if ever, heard on that ship.

The doctor was gloomy, sunken in gloom, he was. Although he had no bad wounds, he said he was badly shaken and pretty sore and not as young as he used to be. Again the silent voice spoke words in Anthony's soul. "Comfort him," it said softly. So Anthony sat down by the doctor and began to speak. He felt foolish, for he had never tried to comfort anyone before and did not know what to say. But the strange thing was that he did not know what he *did* say, but only that the doctor was staring hard at him, and the surliness was fading out of his face. Presently he said, "Somehow, it doesn't sound like *your* voice speaking, lad." And he spoke gently himself.

Next Anthony went into the hold, and there he found the little Chinese cook crying all by himself, his yellow face swollen and his hands with cuts all over them. He was murmuring in his tears of the white flowers and the crystal streams and the saffron skies in his own home. Once again our Lady spoke to Anthony, telling him to lift the little man into his hammock and set about the cooking. This alarmed Anthony, for although he had to help with scraping potatoes and stirring pots, he was no cook, and nothing put out the crew so badly as a poor meal.

But the command persisted, so he got out the pots and pans, and while the Chinaman cried himself to sleep like a child in his hammock, Anthony began to prepare the dinner. Then, again, he caught a glimpse of those tender hands, scouring the pots before starting, moving swiftly and lovingly over the fishes and potatoes, and when he crossed the hold, he heard a lighter but firmer footstep than his own crossing beside him. And the business went forward with unbelievable ease, so that when the first course was in the oven, he thought he would try a pudding for a surprise, for puddings were a rare treat. And when the pudding was done, he went so far as to make a cake for tea and put it away until the time came.

No sooner did the excellent smell of the cooking fill the ship than everyone began to cheer up, and when it was on the table, the dinner worked wonders. "Why," said Jake, "I don't ever remember a dinner on *Bird on the Wing* as good as this. I didn't know Li Chung could do it."

Anthony smiled and said nothing, for, after all, if it was not Li Chung's cooking, neither was it his.

There was often trouble on that ship over the swabbing of the decks and the polishing of the stanchions, for pirates are as ship-proud as other sailors, and Anthony was inexperienced. Most days a few kicks came his way. But now, in a truly wonderful manner, the decks soon became spick and span, and the polishing rag seemed to fly about of itself under his hand. The beauty of their ship seemed to give a new contentment to the pirates.

In the days before our Lady's coming, Anthony had trembled when he was called to the captain's cabin, but now that, too, was different. For one thing, he loved to see the statue and to say a prayer before it. It was even more joyful to see that the captain, too, would sit looking at it, and that it was softening his heart. He would often speak of his little girl, for the thought of giving her the "doll" reminded him of her. To Anthony, the idea of the captain's having a little girl was one that changed him into a different sort of man. He wondered what she was like, and even asked. The captain seemed glad to talk of her. It was plain to all that he was beginning to want to see her again, and to see his home in France, where she lived alone with her old nurse.

Yes, the captain began to talk of home. The others, too, talked of home, and Jake began telling yarns of sailors who did *not* look down into the water and fall a prey to enchantment, but who weathered mighty storms and came at last to harbor and their own hearth.

Day after day, things grew better. But a series of miracles (even small miracles, like a boy's clumsy hands binding wounds deftly, and the dinner being perfect, and beautiful cakes with icing suddenly setting a crew of pirates remembering childhood meals with the mother at the head of the table) cannot pass unnoticed as the things of every day. At first they said, "That lad is improving. The decks look fine. The boy can bind a wound like a nurse."

But after a time, when torn socks and torn shirts were mysteriously mended, and pillows were fluffed up at night and covers smoothed over them in the hammocks, and some gentle breath blew out the lamps and invisible hands trimmed the wick for the morrow, they began to question. A good deal of whispering went on, until it was at last an open secret that in some strange and lovely way the ship was haunted. And they all began to look at the statue and to see for themselves what a warm, mothering look there was about it, in the smiling eyes and mouth, in the kind and sensible hands, in the ample folds of the skirt, even in the way the little golden feet were firmly set on the ground.

Not only was the beautiful ship *Bird on the Wing* haunted, but so were their own hearts. Some spell was calling them home from the sea, home to children and wives and old mothers, and to family meals and kindness and ease. And Jake said, "There is no doubt about it at all, it is the Woman on board." But the captain did not join the talk. He set their course for France.

When they were in sight of shore, the pirates came to the captain, and the doctor was spokesman. "We feel," he said, "that if you are going to leave the little wooden Lady ashore with your daughter, we can sail no more under your flag, for there will be no luck on the ship. Before she came, we were different men. We'd forgotten the good, happy things in life, and it took a mother to bring them to our minds. Ashore we could enjoy our homes, good food, and clean, mended clothes and the pillows fluffed up and cake for dessert; and with the tiny Lady aboard, we can enjoy them here. But without her, the old days would come again: sore heads and bad food and ragged shirts, and all the rest that goes with pirating."

The captain answered, "I am leaving her with my little girl, and I've been thinking it's a sad life the little girl has with no father at home. I'm thinking it's time to settle down. Only I love *Bird on the Wing*, and I can't take her from the sea or give her to any other man. But one thing I can do, and that I will: I'll sail her under a new flag, and I'll sail her honestly in decent trading, for I want to enjoy my home when I go ashore regularly, in peace of mind."

So it came about that, what with the thought of home, and the longing for peace of mind, and a new love for the gracious thing that a mother makes of life, the pirates repented their ways and made their minds up to be shriven on the shores of France.

They hauled down the skull and crossbones and ran up a new flag, a white flag showing a golden lily and a star. Who had made the new flag no one knew.

And when *Bird on the Wing* came through the shining waters into France, the chantey they sang while they dropped her anchors was an old and loving hymn to Our Lady, Star of the Sea.

And our Lady never forsook *Bird on the Wing*, although, in the end, the statue was put into a church that looked over the harbor. For when the beautiful ship had sailed to India and China and many another port, laden with spices and fruit, one day she dropped gently, mysteriously, into English waters once more, bringing Anthony, newly ordained, to live his dream at last, in the country that was his own home.

Jack and Jim

Long ago, when all of England was Catholic, there were two brothers who were twins. Only their mother and people who knew them very well indeed could tell one from the other. They were the same height, and they spoke with what might have been the same voice. One was called Jack (for John), the other Jim (for James). They were nearly always together, and when they had to be apart, even for a short time, they felt strange: each of them felt as if a part of *himself* was missing.

The mother of Jack and Jim was a washer-woman. Washing clothes at that time, although a much harder job than it is now, was a much more beautiful one. The kitchen of the cottage opened on a little garden, and when the mother got the clothes out of her copper tub, she hung them up on a line to dry in the sun. They were beautiful clothes, too, not skimpy and drab as they often are now, but full and gaily colored, and with plenty of white linen among them: wimples, kerchiefs, and so on, which shone out a dazzling white when the sun had bleached them.

Every Saturday afternoon, Jack and Jim took the bundles of clean washing and delivered them to the great houses of the countryside, taking it in turns to go to the castle. The castle was just outside the village, and they loved to go there, because they went through beautiful grounds with swans on lakes of water and with apple orchards; and sometimes they saw brilliantly dressed young pages, or even the noblemen themselves riding about on their horses with hawks on their wrists.

On the way to the castle, there was a roadside crucifix. The twins had known it and loved it ever since they could toddle, for like all English

boys in those days, they had a deep, true love for our Lord and a deep, true pity for His suffering.

But there was one thing about the crucifix that puzzled them: the face was a smiling face. Not the mouth: that was straight and almost grim, carved with a sharpness that was full of pain. And the ribs were showing in five deep lines around the thin, straight body, like five fingers of pain gripping tightly around the heart. But the smile was there, in the curved closed eyes, in the shape of the cheekbones. It seemed to hide in the old, dark wood, polished by the gentle stroking of babies' hands when their mothers held them up to kiss the figure. It was a strange, secret smile, coming from within, from behind the closed eyes, from inside the carved body, as if the heart in the circle of ribs glowed and shone with light, and the light shone through the closed eyes.

"I can't understand," Jim said to Jack, "why our Lord *smiles* on the Cross. I would have thought they would carve Him with tears on His cheeks."

Jack agreed, but added, "All the same, Father Abbot often says in his sermons that our Lord *likes* to suffer for us."

One Saturday Jack came home after delivering his bundles of washing earlier than usual. "Where is Jim?" he asked. "Gone to the castle, dear," said his mother.

"Well," said Jack, "there is nothing to do here, so I'll go and meet him coming back."

When Jack was saying this, Jim was wrestling with a temptation. He was in the castle orchard, and many of the apples on the trees were ripe and rosy and very good to look at. Mother had told them, "Never, never must you touch the fruit in other people's gardens," but these apples seemed to be crying out to be eaten. You had only to look at them to know they were sweet and hard and crisp to the teeth. You had only to look at one to know that the sun had entered into the very core of it to ripen it and warm it through to the peel.

Jim looked desperately at the grass. Perhaps there would be windfalls, and he thought there could be no harm in taking those. But some page must have been there before him, for there were none to be seen. No harm, he thought, just to touch one. He put out his hand, and somehow or other, the apple he touched came gently into his hand. And in a few more seconds, not only that one, but several others were hidden inside his tunic.

A few minutes later, he had delivered his bundle and was ready to go home. And then those apples began to burn in his tunic, making his conscience smolder with shame and fear. He wanted to throw them down on the grass, but he was afraid that he might be seen. Then it would be known that he had stolen them, and perhaps they would not let his mother do the castle washing anymore, because her son was a thief. He decided to go around another way so that he could get out of the castle grounds quickly. And then, he thought, when he was on the other side of the wall and could not be seen, he would toss the apples over the wall.

As a matter of fact, Jim *had* been seen. When he took the apples, an old gardener had been lying in the orchard taking a nap in the sun. Jim's footsteps had wakened him, and, lying among the grass and trees, he had seen the boy without being seen. Now he meant to let him have it, and he stood waiting for him to pass by on his way home. He was waiting just when Jack, knowing nothing of all this, came along the path.

Jack walked briskly. In fact, he came like a dog, giving little runs every so often, and every now and then jumping up in the air. He whistled, too, and in every way looked (and for that matter was) jaunty and conscience-free. All this seemed to the gardener to be the very sign of a hardened young sinner. If Jack had come along as Jim was just then walking, he would have felt sorry for him. For Jim was still red with shame and was walking slowly, close beside the castle wall, every now and then looking over his shoulder.

The gardener jumped out suddenly from behind a tree and barred Jack's way. "Caught you!"

he shouted. "You thought you had gotten away, didn't you? But I saw you, you thieving young rascal. I saw you taking apples from the tree and hiding them in your coat."

Jack opened his mouth to say, "I never did such a thing!" when suddenly the truth rushed over him. The old man had seen Jim do it. And this truth was like a wave of shame sweeping over Jack.

"D'you know what I'll do?" shouted the gardener. "I'll take you to the count, that I will," and he went on with such a scorching tirade as Jack had never heard before, full of very cruel words and threats, each more awful than the last.

But, as Jack listened in silence, a strange sort of gladness came over him. Whatever the old man might do, he would do to *him*, not to Jim; and he would gladly bear it to save Jim.

Of course it was awful for Jim to steal the apples, but Jack knew that he would be sorry by now. And he was glad, very glad, that he could take the blame.

He felt tears pricking his eyes, and he could not speak because his throat felt suddenly too big and sore. But as he stood there and the old man's words fell on him and bruised him like a shower of sharp stones, he felt that his love for his brother, grown inside him, was in a secret way like a flower. He felt he was somehow holding Jim's heart up and taking his shame away, and that it would be easy for him to take the punishment, whatever it might be.

Suddenly the gardener stopped. His voice changed. He put his hand on Jack's shoulder. "Why, laddie," he said, "you do take a scolding well. You're not insolent, like some of those saucy pages. Now cheer up. I've given you your medicine, and that'll do. You can be off!" Then, as Jack was going, he shouted, "Here, catch!" and tossed him a couple of huge red apples.

It chanced that the twins met just by the wayside crucifix. Jim must have heard part of the gardener's tirade. The little trees that grew about the cross made a green gloom mixed with a golden light; and in this light the face of the figure on the cross glowed and seemed to smile more visibly than usual.

"Hullo!" said Jack.

"Hullo!" said Jim.

"Have an apple," said Jack. "The old gardener gave it to me."

"No, thanks," said Jim and turned scarlet.

"Oh, come on, stupid, it's mine — " Then Jack said suddenly, "I know why our Lord smiles on the Cross. It's because He is our brother, and He's glad to take away our sins and our shame and our punishments."

Jim was silent for a good time. Finally, he kissed the stiff wooden feet. Then he held out his hand for the apple.

Racla the Gypsy

The gypsies lived in little drab tents, outside the village. Sometimes they pitched their tents in the plains, sometimes in the forest. Theirs was a hard life, wandering through the countryside of Romania. They did not travel, as gypsies often do, in painted caravans, but carrying great water pots on their backs, with perhaps one or two old scraggy horses or a tired old ox to help them with the tents and pots and pans.

Racla had wandered thus through many villages and towns and had seen glimpses of many strange and lovely things. Over and over again in the churches, where the gypsies went to keep warm or to beg, he had seen the icon of the kind old Father God, and he liked Him. The long, white beard seemed to him like a good blanket, or like the sheepskins that the gypsies tied around their heads to keep winter frost from biting their ears, and anything warm that you could wrap around you seemed good to Racla. And he liked the stiff jeweled clothes that God wore, and His crown, and the way He lifted up His hands as though He were throwing roubles to the poor.

When they pitched their tents far from the houses, and came to anchor for some long time, planting a little wheat seed and waiting for it to grow up into bread, Racla was sorry, because he would not see the picture of God again until they wandered on.

One day Father Filipesco came from the village to the camp, and Racla thought that he was God. Father Filipesco, too, had a long white beard and slanting kind eyes, and he lifted his hand in the same way, but he threw very few roubles, for he was poor. As soon as a rich stranger came their way, the gypsy children turned cartwheels and

stood on their heads to earn a few coins. Racla stood on his head before Father Filipesco, because he thought he was God, and when the others had grabbed the few coins the old priest had, he still stayed upside down in the act of worship. For although he knew very little, he knew that when God comes to visit us, we adore Him.

Father Filipesco sat down on a tree stump and laughed. And when he laughed, his beard heaved up and down like sea foam in a storm, and the gold cross on his great chest flashed in the sun, and he beat his knees with the hands that had so few coins to give. And little Racla, who had never before had such high praise for his cartwheels and capers, glowed all over. He even dared to come close to the kind, laughing God and smile at him.

The priest drew Racla to his knee and began to talk to him. "Stop your capers," he said, "for I have no more money."

Racla said, "But for God I will do it without money, and you are God."

"I am not God, but His poor servant," said Father Filipesco. "I try to be like Him and to teach His sheep what He is like."

"Is that why you have a beard like a blanket of wool?"

"Maybe, but it is more in my heart than my beard that I try to be like Him." He told Racla how God is a Spirit living in the hearts of His little ones, and how they can learn to be like Him by doing as Christ did on earth. Racla knew nothing of that, but Father Filipesco came again and baptized him and began to tell him the story of our Lord. And Racla, who had never before known anyone who loved him and told him stories, loved the old priest more than you or I can dream of.

For a long time, all was well. Heaven had broken in Racla's heart like white blossoms on a spring day. And then a cloud came.

The cloud was Rosa. In the village, the peasants worked for the master of the big house. They were cared for by him like children and were paid, not in gold, but in bread and sugar and tobacco, rolls of cloth, little homes — indeed, all they could want. And the master had a little girl called Rosa. She was beautiful, and she was dressed in silk. Her hair was soft, and she had shining beads around her neck and wrists, and Father Filipesco loved her as he loved Racla. Racla knew this, for he often went into the village and saw Rosa run out of the gates of the big house to greet the Father, and the old priest smiled as kindly at her as he did at Racla.

The boy was jealous. Out in the plains, when they were alone together, it seemed easy to understand that God has so big a heart that He loves *all* His creatures, even the lean horses and the tumbledown ox, even Rosa; and that we who are like Him must love them all, too. Yes, it was easy enough when Father Filipesco came with one or two pieces of candy and a rouble and gave that and his lovely words and laughter to Racla alone; but in the village, when Rosa was lifted up in his friend's arms and made much of, it was not easy. Something black turned round and round in his heart, and he scowled through the big gates at Rosa.

One day a servant from the big house chased him away, and he heard Rosa say, "We can't have gypsies hanging around," and after that he thought that he almost hated her.

"She has everything," Racla said to Father Filipesco. "Her clothes are silk. She has flashing jewels. She has a big house. She doesn't need to have you."

"Racla," said Father Filipesco, "she has less than you, for her heart is full of things that pass away, while yours is empty, and God can fill it. She is a spoiled little girl, and it is not as easy for her to be like God as it is for you. He was like you, wandering from place to place, so poor that when He died, He had not a grave of His own, and even His clothes were taken from Him, and when, just before He died, He wanted to have supper with His friends, He had to ask someone to lend Him a room for it."

And he told the story of Christ in the Upper Room, how He sat with the few men who loved Him and comforted them because they were heavy with sorrow. And how, as the sun went down behind His head, and the day passed as His life on earth was soon to pass, He told them that He would live in them and they should all be one — all love each other, all be at peace with one another, as He was one with His Father and at peace in Him. And then blessing the bread, He changed it into His Body, into Himself, and gave it to them.

"And I will give it to you," said Father Filipesco. "But you must be at peace in your heart, and with Rosa!"

But it was not Father Filipesco who gave the Bread of Christ to Racla, for only a few days after he had told him that last tender story of Christ, he was taken suddenly from this life and went to dwell forever with the God whom he had shown to Racla. The funeral procession was followed by many who wept, and yet it was not wholly sad, for all the people carried candles in their hands, and the priest's coffin seemed like a small boat carried on a river of light to rest. And they sang very sweetly, the voices of the gypsies richer than the rest. For because the gypsies live harder lives, but lives closer to the wild things of God, they fear death less; their voices had more of joy mingled in the sadness than the others.

In front of the coffin, a huge cake was carried, a cake for which (despite the tears on his cheeks) many a small boy's mouth was watering. In Romania, when a man is laid to rest, waiting the rising of his body, his last deed is one of loving kindness. The funeral cake is cut at the side of his grave, as a bridal cake at a marriage, and given to the poor. The body in the grave hungers no more, but his last deed is homely and kind: a cake to feed the hungry.

Rosa was given none of the cake, for it is only for the poor. She stood still and pale, holding her nurse's hand, looking very miserable and sad, and Racla for the first time was sorry for her.

He put his own cake into his shirt, over his heart; he did not want to eat it. It was all he had now to hold on to, all that he had of Father Filipesco which he could touch and feel. He began to understand better why Christ left His Body to men to be touched by them and taken close to them, why He chose *that* way of giving Himself to them to live in their souls.

And Rosa had none of the cake! He pressed it closer under his shirt. How lovely it was; it seemed to tell him that Father Filipesco still cared for him. The others were eating theirs, and they were cheering up, talking and laughing on their way. Racla, too, felt happy. He would go to the new priest who would come, and ask for the Bread that is Christ, and when he grew up, he would have a big beard like a blanket and a kind heart like the priest who was dead, and he would show God to gypsy boys.

But Rosa had no cake! That went on in his mind like a sad little song. And perhaps she did not understand as he did. And if Christ shared

Himself, even Himself, with everyone, should he not share his cake with Rosa? Should he not, if he was going to be given Christ in the bread?

He went back to the village and through the gates of the big house. Perhaps they would drive him away again because he was a gypsy, but he would try. He would say that he was Father Filipesco's friend; he would pray to Father Filipesco to help him.

It was the master of the house who met him in the drive, and he listened kindly to what the boy told him. Then taking his hand, he said very gently, "You shall come with me to Rosa, and you shall eat the cake with her. But what shall we do for you, who are so kind with God's kindness? Do you want clothes or roubles or beads?"

Racla shook his head, for suddenly those things seemed nothing. He only wanted to be like the priest, like God in the icon, like God with the lifted, empty hands that give all things.

The Shepherd's Coat

There was never anyone else in the world who could tell such beautiful stories as Benji's grandfather. And of all the stories he told, none was so wonderful as the true story of the night when he went to the cave in Bethlehem and saw the mysterious Baby. He loved to tell it again and again. When the sheep were all in the fold and no lamb straying, he would gather the younger shepherds and the lads around him and tell them the tale.

He would describe the sudden glory and the choirs of angels shouting their joyful song, and the great ropes of stars swinging like golden chains in the sky — and in their midst, one great solitary star that was more beautiful than all the others put together.

But when it came to the part about seeing the little family in the stable, the Infant lying in the manger, the poor father, and the very young mother, then the old man's voice shook as if he were near to tears, as if this memory were too sweet for him.

Most of the shepherds laughed kindly, for it seemed funny to them that an old man should be more stirred by three ordinary people in a stable than by a sky blazing with angels. Benji understood, but he kept wondering why the angels took the shepherds to see this child. And when the others had wrapped their blankets around them and gone to sleep, Benji would ask Grandfather questions long into the night. "Did you give Him anything?"

"Yes, Benji, a little lambskin, for the poor mite was shivering."

"How long ago was it?"

"It was twelve years ago."

"So now He would be my age, a boy like me?"

"Yes."

"Grandfather, He must be *somewhere*. Do you think we could ever find Him again?"

"Well, I don't think so, Benji. When we went back, they had gone. The stable was empty except for the four-footed beasts. But I do remember a strange thing: along with the smell of newly cut hay and the warmth of the cattle, there was a smell of incense and sweet spices, myrrh and spikenard."

"How I wish I knew who He was, and where He is," said Benji.

One day Benji's father gave him a sheepskin coat. "You are twelve years old," he said. "That is grown up, and now you must be a real shepherd." He put the sheepskin coat on him and the shepherd's crook in his hand. When Benji felt the warmth and softness of the coat, and saw how the sheep came up close to him and huddled against it, he began to understand the sheep in a new way, and all that it meant to be a shepherd.

Every morning now, he opened the fold to let out the flock on the hills, and every evening he gathered them home. And often, as he did so, he wondered where that Boy was who had been an infant in the manger. Benji thought, "If only I could find out where He is and go to Him, I would give Him my sheepskin coat, the best thing I have. Yes, I would kneel down and put it on Him and fasten the belt around His waist, and I would serve Him forever and ever." And when the sheep were penned, he would pray to God under the stars, "Grant to me, mighty Father, that I may find the wonderful little one and may give Him my sheepskin coat."

One windy evening, with a gale coming up and a dark scud of clouds driving across the sky, a lamb was discovered missing. Benji had to find it. As he shut the little wicket of the fold, "Be good," he said to the sheep, who were huddled together, afraid of the coming storm. "Be good. You need not be afraid in the pen, but your baby brother is lost, and I must look for him; he may be stuck in a thornbush or be on a dangerous cliff. I must go and find him."

The hills seemed empty and the sky now like the roof of an empty vault, and the wind was howling. It was hard to know where to look for the lamb. Benji tried first one path, then another, and every so often he stood listening for its little bleat.

At last he thought that he heard it, a poor little frightened wail down the wind. "I'm coming," he shouted. "Where are you?" He hoped the lamb would bleat again to direct him. To his amazement words came back, a tiny shrill voice saying, "Here I am! I'm lost!"

Benji followed the voice along a craggy path, and coming around the corner of a big rock, he saw, not his lamb, but a tiny boy, shivering with cold and fear and weeping pitifully. "I'm lost; I'm cold; I'm hungry," he wept.

Benji knelt down and put his arm around him. "I will take you home when I've found my lamb," he said. "Tell me where you live."

But the little boy was sobbing now in a way that he could not stop. His poor little ribs were heaving in and out, and his teeth were chattering. Suddenly an idea came to Benji. He took off his sheepskin coat and put it on the little boy. It was all warm with the warmth of Benji's own body, and as soon as the little boy felt the comfort of it, he began to stop crying.

When at last the lamb was found, and Benji had taken the lost child to his own door, he had not the heart to take back his coat. He seemed to be such a poor little boy, and his own coat was so thin. His mother was a poor woman, and Benji thought, "For a shepherd, it is easy to get such a coat, but for this boy, it would mean having a big sum of money to buy it. I will let him keep mine."

As he went home without his coat, clasping the found lamb, he felt sad. He was not sad not to have the coat for himself anymore, but he suddenly remembered that now, if he ever saw the wonderful Boy of the angels' song, he could not give Him his first shepherd's coat. And no other one would be the same, for this first coat had been the sign of his being a shepherd, and it had made him friends with the flock. He felt almost as though he had given *himself* to the little lost boy!

The day came when Grandfather was too old to live out on the hills, and Benji, who was now nearly thirty years old, took him down to Jerusalem to live with some of his relations within the shadow of the Temple walls. They went by way of Mount Olivet, and as they climbed to the top and the city of Jerusalem came into sight, they saw a group of people sitting on the ground talking, very much as the shepherds themselves often sat talking on the hillside. A few women also were standing near. Below them in the valley, surrounded by the sunset clouds, lay Jerusalem, and in the midst of it the Temple, like the jewel in a gold ring.

Benji had eyes only for the city and might not have even noticed the people on the hillside at all, if Grandfather had not suddenly gripped his arm and whispered in his ear, "Benji, Benji, it is the Infant of Bethlehem!"

Benji looked around in astonishment. There were just a few poor men there, and one in the midst of them explaining something, a young Man of about his own age. It was at this Man his grandfather was looking so intently. But how could he possibly know?

"How do you know?" he asked.

"Why, do you not see that woman watching Him? Do you see her face, and the love in her face? Do you see it, Benji?"

"Yes, I do."

"Well, Benji, isn't it sure that she is the young Man's mother?"

"It is, indeed, Grandfather. That's a mother's look, I'm sure."

"Well then, Benji, it's the Baby the angels led us to, for I recognize her; she is the mother who was in the stable. I know Him by His mother."

Then Benji's heart leapt up in joy and love. "O Grandfather," he said, "if only I still had my first sheepskin coat, the only *great* treasure that I ever had. It was my dream to give it to Him, but I went and gave it away to a cold little stranger I found when I was looking for one of our lambs!"

"Hush, lad!" said Grandfather. "Let us listen to what He's saying. For He is surely the Lord." They moved a little closer and listened.

The Lord was speaking slowly, as He looked at the listeners. To the delight of the shepherds,

He was speaking about sheep. He was saying, "And He shall set the sheep on His right hand, and the goats on His left."

The two shepherds stood like statues, hardly wanting to breathe, lest they fail to hear the beautiful voice. And the voice went on telling what we have often heard, but what they were hearing for the first time, how on the Day of Judgment, people would find out with astonishment that little kind things they had done and forgotten were really done to the Lord, who would never forget.

"I was naked," Benji heard, "and you covered me." He listened intently, and the lovely story went on until the Lord said that the people would ask, "Lord, when did we see Thee naked and cover Thee?" And the answer came back, "As long as you did it to one of these, my least brethren, you did it to me."

Just then the Lord looked aside and smiled at Benji, and suddenly Benji saw a cold little boy cuddled in the sheepskin coat again, and he understood. It was as if a peal of joyous bells were ringing in his soul.

There was not a word spoken. Benji went back to his sheep and lived the life of a good shepherd. But he knew that his dream had come true. And he knew now that it came true long before he had seen the Child, whom the angels sang for, grown to be a Man.

Joseph's Godfather

If the bomb hadn't fallen in the next street over, Joseph might never have known his godfather. For, to tell the truth, he was a very bad godfather indeed. He had never even asked whether Joseph had made his First Communion, let alone sent him a birthday present, or even a postcard. Then, just before the bomb fell, Mother received a letter. She read it out loud, and they all laughed:

Dear Margaret,

I suppose you know that I now live in England at the above address. You had better send your child to me for the duration.

Arthur

Mother made excuses for him, but, then, she always made excuses for everyone. "He has been shooting tigers in India for years," she said, "miles from a church, and so I am afraid he has become a little odd. He may even have given up going to Mass."

"That's a fine sort of godfather for me," said Joseph.

"You must pray for him," Mother answered.

And then, the very next night, the bomb fell. "That settles it," said Mother. "Joseph must accept his godfather's invitation."

"What!" said Joseph. "Go and live until the war ends with an old man who is odd and doesn't even go to Mass?"

"You are ten years old," Mother answered, "and a soldier's son, old enough to go to Mass and act sensibly yourself. And you must pray for your godfather. Of course, it's going to be hard. You may feel very lonely and strange at first. Godfather is used to being treated like a little tin god in India. He won't like any fresh answers, you know, but you must be brave and act like a man. Try to offer it all up for Godfather."

The afternoon when Joseph arrived at his godfather's house was the unhappiest one he had ever spent. Although the cook was kind and motherly and sat him down to a nice supper by the kitchen stove, Joseph had a sinking feeling in his stomach. The food turned to ashes in his mouth, and he felt the tears he was determined not to shed making his throat sore.

"What's Godfather like?" he asked miserably.

Before Cook could answer anything, Singh, the Indian manservant, who was cleaning a pair of Godfather's shoes, answered, "He is a very fine gentleman, *pukka Sahib*."

"What's that?"

"Bless your heart!" said Cook. "You don't know what a *pukka Sahib* is? Why, it means a great gentleman, and that's just what the general is."

"Is Godfather a general?"

Singh said proudly, "He is a *great* general. Soldiers tremble when he speaks; tigers run away."

Just then the bell rang, and Singh went to answer it. He came back for Joseph. "The general wants to see you," he said.

Joseph took hold of Singh's hand and held it until they got to the door. He felt much more frightened than he did of bombs, and he longed for Mother.

At the door he said, "I'll go in alone."

It was as bad as he expected. His godfather stood before the fire on a tiger-skin rug, a tall, straight, white-haired, bristling old gentleman with a mustache twisted into spikes like two daggers, a monocle in one eye, a very large, very red nose, and eyebrows that bristled out over his fierce blue eyes like the antennae that Joseph had photographs of in his nature books.

"How do you do, sir?" said Joseph politely.

"How do I do, eh? Ha! That's a good one. How do *I* do?" Godfather gave a roar of savage laughter, and Joseph, who could not see anything funny in his greeting, trembled. "How do *I* do? Ah, ah, ah! I do fine, I take good care I do. How do *you* do? That's the point. Let's see you. Come here."

"Thank you, sir. I'm very well."

"Stuff and nonsense, don't answer me back! Very well! Upon my word, you look half-starved." He screwed his monocle so tightly into his eye that it looked as if he were grinding it into his face, and peered more closely at Joseph. "I've never seen such a weedy child," he shouted. "You look like something someone grew in a cellar, a white radish, or a carrot someone pulled up too soon. I suppose you don't take any exercise, eh? Play polo?"

"Play what, sir?"

"Polo. Are you deaf? Don't you ride horses?"

"No, sir."

"Frightened of 'em, eh?"

"No, sir."

"Don't answer me back, I tell you. I wouldn't put up with it from a tiger or a cannibal or from a regiment of soldiers. Bah! It's mutiny, that's what it is!"

Joseph soon got friendly with Cook and the Indian, Singh, and had plenty of fun riding the pony. And although Godfather roared and spluttered at him, he gave him presents every day, didn't send him to school, and let him stay up late for dinner. In fact, he spoiled Joseph so much that he began to be fresh to Cook and to quarrel with Singh (although he was his greatest friend), to be choosy about his food, and worst of all, to find it really rather boring to say his prayers. One day he had to say to himself, "I'm being a rotten Catholic!" and he resolved to make sacrifices for Godfather and to make sure by keeping a list of them. "That will make me do it, or else," he said. He asked Cook if Godfather ever went to Mass.

"Bless you, he hasn't set foot in church many a year," she said.

The rest of this story has to be told from the general's point of view. To tell you the truth, he liked Joseph better every day, and one day he was looking out the window, watching him ride his pony and feeling rather proud of him, when he caught sight of what he thought was Cook's shopping list dropped on the floor. He picked it up and started to read it. He frowned, twirled his mustache, stared, said, "What the —? Why the —!" and read it all over again.

"Sacrifices for Godfather, to convert him," he read. "Didn't answer back. Ate stewed pears, which I hate. Didn't have lemonade, which I love."

The next day Joseph found Singh and Cook worried. "The Master's sick," said Singh. "He's gone mad."

"And wouldn't touch a nice, little chicken I served for his supper last night," said Cook.

"And him drinking cold water, not whiskey and soda," said Singh.

"Take his shoes to him," Cook said, "and ask him where he hurts."

Singh was gone a long time. He came back more worried than ever. "Master's gone mad," he said sadly. "I dropped the best Chinese china dog and broke it. The Master, he turned red, he opened his mouth to roar, and no roar came out. He shut his mouth, struggled as if he had a pain, and said nothing at all!"

"*You* go, Joseph," said Cook, and she began dabbing her eyes and sniffing. "Sounds as if his end is coming."

Joseph went straight up to Godfather's chair. He was not nervous of him now.

"Godfather," he said, "please tell me what's up. Cook and Singh think you are dying. You aren't eating chicken or drinking whiskey and soda, and you aren't swearing and shouting or anything. If you're dying, you'd better call for the priest, because we love you, and we don't want you to go to Hell."

All of a sudden, Godfather began to laugh, but not very loud. It was more like giggling, and his face looked like that of a little boy who has been caught in something silly. He got Joseph's sacrifice list, all crumpled up, out of his breast pocket, smoothed it out on his knee, and said, "See this?"

Joseph did, and he turned as red as a geranium. "Yes, sir," he said.

"Well, I've been trying to see if I could do, for myself, as much as *you* are doing for me. You see? I think it's very decent of you, and, by Jove, boy, I can't keep it up! I haven't even started on stewed pears; the things make me sick. Ugh! Why, tigers and cannibals are easy to keep down compared with the old Adam in me. I give it to you, Joseph. You've got more pluck than I have."

"Oh, no, sir," Joseph said, "what rot. I mean, sir, I'm awfully sorry; it's *not* rot. But you see, I can do sacrifices because I go to Confession and Communion, and so our Lord is in my soul and He helps me. I couldn't do them myself, *by* myself — not even easy ones, as those are!"

"Easy! By gad, *easy!*" Poor Godfather had bellowed again. He clapped his hand over his mouth.

That evening Joseph went to Confession. He got there early and was first in the line. It was a fairly long one, and when he came out, he saw something very surprising. The last one in the line was Godfather. He was crouching down looking rather funny, like a naughty boy again, with the collar of his coat turned up around his ears. Joseph pretended not to see him, but after his penance, he said a huge thanksgiving.

That night, when Joseph, very brushed and washed, came in to dinner, he was surprised to see that there were silver bowls of flowers on the table and everything spread for a feast. Godfather was beaming. He was pouring out some lemonade for Joseph.

"Joseph," he said, "tonight we are having a little celebration. I've been and done it: gone to Confession, by Jove. I feel a different man. So I am, too. We'll have stewed pears another day; it's a feast tonight."

And what a feast it was! First, Singh came in grinning with fried chicken on a silver dish. Then he brought in a bowl heaped high with a mound of mashed potatoes, a pat of rich, yellow butter melting in the middle, and fresh green peas from Cook's garden. Cook had baked her special biscuits, large and crisp, and had made a salad of apples, nuts, and grapes. But best of all was the dessert: a feathery-light angel-food cake with chocolate icing and three kinds of ice cream: strawberry, chocolate, and vanilla.

The Anchoress

The little king was very sad. He sat in the turret of his great gloomy castle and peered over his kingdom, or at least as much of it as he could see. Far away in the distance he could see woods and fields, very small from so far off, like little painted fields and trees, painted blue and green. And then he leaned right out and looked down at the streets that wound around the castle, and at all the twisted chimneys and the gabled houses, and at the birds' nests in the gables. He thought, "How friendly the chimneys are; they are always two leaning together; there is never one little one alone."

And he leaned out further still, until he could see the boys playing in the street. They looked funny, because he saw them from above. Their heads looked round and dark, and when they passed right under him, he could see the round head and the clogged feet only, no body in between, so that they looked like balls with feet. "How happy they are," he sighed. "They are not like me, all alone because I am a king."

But he leaned so far out of the window that my Lord Cardinal, who had been watching him all the time, drew him in by the heels. "Your Majesty must be robed for the procession now," he said.

The king stamped his foot; he was weary of processions, weary of kingship. "I will not lead it, my Lord Cardinal. I am tired of being king. It is all processions and receptions and lessons. I have had enough. Make some other boy king. I will stay here today."

My Lord Cardinal looked gently at him. "Nay, do not strive against God's will. He it is who has made you king. It is a wearisome thing for a little boy, but we all find God's will for us tedious sometimes." He bent down, smiling, and whispered into the king's ear, "It is a wearisome thing sometimes to be a cardinal; it would often be a great joy to wear the shoes of the old priest in the town, who plays with the boys in the street."

"I will be king no more," raged the boy. "Today I will stay here. I hate my processions." But my Lord Cardinal took his hand and led him to his robing room.

That night the king fell to turning somersaults and was scolded by the royal tutor. "Do you not know," he said, "that you are the Lord's anointed?"

And he bore the Lord's anointed, struggling and screaming with temper, to the highest turret of all and locked him in for punishment. This turret was quite empty. It was very seldom used, since the king was seldom punished. But of late his tantrums had become unbearable to the whole court.

The turret was quite empty, or so it seemed at first, and it was growing dark, for there was only a slit for a window. But presently the king heard a twittering in the corner, and there, built right into the wall, was a nest of young birds. The king sat very still and watched them, and presently through the slit came their mother, flying with a crumb of bread in her mouth.

"Where did you get that crumb?" asked the king, for he knew that his people were very poor and scarcely had bread for themselves.

"From the anchoress," said the bird, and although it was dusk, she broke into a merry little singing.

"Who is the anchoress?" said the king.

"Oh, well," said the bird, "she is the anchoress, just the anchoress," and away she flew, into the dusk again.

The next time she came through the slit, she bore a golden straw in her beak. "That is for my nest," she sang.

"Who gave you the straw?" asked the king.

"The anchoress," said the bird.

"*Who* is the anchoress?" shouted the king.

The bird put her head on one side and thought. Then she put it on the other side and thought again. Then she hopped round and round, thinking harder still.

"Oh dear, oh dear," she twittered, "I've been thinking so hard for the answer that I have forgotten the question!"

"Who is the anchoress?" said the king.

"Oh, yes! The anchoress. That's who she is."

Presently the royal tutor unlocked the door and led the king to his chapel for night prayers. He was not at all pious, but he knelt in his stall with his hands folded on his cushion of red plush and the arms of his family blazoned in gold on the great flag hanging behind him, and he looked very prayerful. He had learned that he must kneel straight and close his eyes, but all the time he was thinking about the little twisty streets winding around the castle. "I don't expect *those* boys have to say their prayers," he thought. But out loud he said, "Amen," and then his page, bearing a long taper, led him to bed.

When the king lay in his silken sheets, his bright hair flowing over the pillow, the door opened softly and my Lord Cardinal crept in. "I have a rosy apple for Your Majesty," he said.

The king sat bolt upright. "Be seated, my Lord," he said, and the old man sat on his bed. "Tell me a story," said the king. "But no, tell me instead, who is the anchoress?"

My Lord Cardinal lifted the king into his arms and carried him to the window. The streets were all dark, and the chimneys huddled together against a pale sky. Far away beyond the houses, one little light burned, like a single star, in a turret that stood against the church. "Do you see that light?"

"That is her light. The anchoress is a lady who lives all alone in a turret that has no door, only one little window through which men pass her bread and water. That window looks on the world, on all the poverty and sickness and sin, and on all the riches and foolishness that pass the window. And, inside, another little window looks into the church, on all the treasure and healing and holiness and all the sacrifice and wisdom of Heaven."

"How silly of her to live alone in that turret," said the king. "She could be free and run in the street."

My Lord Cardinal put the king back to bed. "I could not make Your Majesty understand," he said, "not yet. One day it may be that our Lord Christ will make you wise. Now eat your apple and go to sleep. God bless you, little son."

There was a hue and cry in the castle. During the night, the king had vanished! Except for the core of an apple, the royal bed was empty. Pages ran to and fro wringing their hands. Heralds went out blowing great blasts on their trumpets in the streets. The ministers gathered together in council. The soldiers stood in a row with their swords in their hands. And no one had any idea of what to do next. The royal wardrobe was examined, but none of his suits were missing. The pages were forced to think, with a blush of shame, that the king was somewhere, where they knew not, clothed only in a shirt and his long hose. Further search proved that he was unwashed.

When the king slipped out of the great gate, he ran as fast as his legs could carry him to the other end of the town. When he dared to stop and look around, he found himself in a poor street where the little houses were so old that they were leaning on one another for comfort, and all the doors were crooked. In this street, a lot of boys were playing leapfrog. At first the king wondered why they did not bow to him and stop playing; then his heart leaped for joy. "I'm never going to be a king again," he said to himself.

Suddenly the boys saw him, and they began to laugh at him. One of them came up and asked him who he was.

"No one," said the king. "Can I play with you?"

"Why have you got no coat?" said a little girl.

The king flushed. He suddenly understood that he looked very odd and that they were all laughing at him. He was beginning to be hungry

for his breakfast, too. Then from a long way off he heard the sound of the trumpets, and he knew that they were searching for him.

"Please, please hide me!" he cried, but the children ran away.

He knocked, although very timidly, on a door. It opened, and a woman let him in.

"Who are you?" she asked.

"I don't know." The king hung his head; he dared not say who he was. The woman had five children, and they crowded around him. "He must be lost," said one.

"He has no coat," said another.

"He doesn't know who he is," said a third.

The fourth could say only "Mama," and the fifth could not say anything.

"Poor thing," said the woman. "He is shivering cold." She looked around for a coat. " 'Tis a pity we have no coal to light a bit of fire for him. Has anyone a coat?"

The eldest boy took off his own and put it on him, and the king's arms stuck out of it at the elbows because it was so worn; but he was glad of its warmth. One of the little girls gave him some clogs, but they hurt his feet, and the kind woman gave him a piece of black bread and some warm milk. When he had eaten, he went into the street with the five children, and they began to play leapfrog; but he stumbled in his heavy clogs and fell whenever he tried to run.

Suddenly the trumpets blared out again. They were near now. The king stood still and listened.

A man ran down the street. "Make way," he shouted, sweeping them all aside with his arms. "Make way. The king is lost." And he pushed the king over into the gutter and hurried on, shouting the news. All the doors were flung open; heads shot out of every window; people ran out of the houses. The king was lost among them! But the eyes of the boy whose coat he wore were fixed on him; they traveled from the silken hose to the fine golden hair, and suddenly the boy drew away from him as if he were afraid. The king knew that he had guessed. He turned and ran.

When the sun had gone down, the king crept out from under a low archway, where he had hidden nearly all day, and looked around him. He was stiff and cold and hungry. He found that he had run a long way, to the very outskirts of the town, and looking up, he saw that he stood under the turret where the anchoress dwelt. It was a little turret and built not very high. He suddenly thought he would climb up and speak to her; perhaps she would not fear him. He took his clogs off and scrambled up. Her window was crossed with bars, and he was able to hold on to them, and pushing his feet into a crevice in the wall, he peered in.

The anchoress didn't see him. She was a very little lady, clothed like a nun, and she was kneeling with her back turned, looking through the window into the church. And through that window, another little King looked back at her. He was very small. A heavy crown of gold was pressing another crown of thorns on His forehead. A great chasuble weighted with jewels was covering His slender little body. He had put His hands through the bars for the anchoress to hold, and she was kissing them because they were wounded.

Then the earthly king heard the other King speak: "Tell me a story," He said, in a child's voice.

The anchoress laughed low and sweetly; her laughter was very tender. "But Your Majesty knows that I know only one, and You have heard it so often."

"I want to hear it again!"

"Oh, my Love, how patient You are! Do You want to hear yet again the story of the King's Son, who came disguised as a poor boy to win the heart of a beggar maid, because she would have run away if she had seen Him in His royal splendor?"

"Yes, that one," said the thorn-crowned Boy.

The other little boy listening was astonished. It was the story that was written in all his fairy books, and he had heard it over and over again; only now, for the first time, he knew it was true!

At the end of the story, the anchoress turned around and saw the other listener. She smiled at him, and the earthly king asked her, "Who is He?" She crossed the room to him, where he was clinging to the window that opened into the world.

"He is the King," she said. "Do you not see His crown? He is the King of Heaven and earth, but no one seems to want Him. He is so much alone. They don't understand His human Heart that longs for other boys to come and be with

Him. Sometimes they come, but more often He is left alone, and all the sound of the world's sin and sorrow comes in through the window to Him, all day, all night!"

"Can't He go away?"

"Yes," the anchoress said, "but He will not. You see, He loves them. All the poor silly people are His subjects, so He stays here to be among them. And you know His friends understand, and some of them, like me, live alone, too, so that instead of the sound of sad things, He can sometimes be with His friends and hear lovely stories."

The voice of the anchoress grew faint and sounded far away, like the clear sound of a tiny stream flowing in a rock, and the king suddenly found himself taken by the heels and brought down into the cardinal's arms. The cardinal was dressed as an ordinary priest, a black cloak covering him, a broad black hat on his head. The king and the cardinal looked at each other and laughed.

"All day I sought Your Majesty, and many a boy I played with in the street," said my Lord Cardinal. And then softly, "Was it a great day for *you, too*, my dear king?"

Back in the castle, the king, clothed again in his royal robes, the cardinal in his scarlet, the king said, "My Lord Cardinal, tell me that old story."

"Are you not weary of it?"

"No."

The king fell asleep listening, and my Lord Cardinal said to the little bird who perched on the window's ledge with a golden straw in her beak, "We are all in our place, all alone with our Lord, each of us: you in your nest, I in my scarlet, the king in his robes, the poor boy in the street. If we try to be good, we are all little anchorites telling the story of our life to the King to comfort Him."

A Boy in Siberia

A few years ago, a boy of ten, called Vaslav, lived in a forest in Siberia. He was the son of one of the prison guards, a kind man who was good to the prisoners and let them do things that were forbidden to them, such as secretly saying Mass (for many of them were priests). He did not even mind when his son Vaslav was baptized a Christian and started being made ready for his First Communion by a priest-prisoner. "But don't dare tell anyone else," was all he said, "for if you do, we shall all be in serious trouble."

Not all the guards were so easygoing. One of them, Andreyev, a big, strong young man, hated Christians, not because they had ever hurt him, but because ever since he was a little boy, he had been taught lies about them. He was told that they were cruel and hard to children and to the poor. He himself was very kind to the poor and loved children; in fact, he had all the qualities in him that might have made him a saint, if he had only known the truth about Jesus Christ.

One day a whisper went around that Mass was going to be celebrated in the forest. Someone had smuggled in some white bread; someone else a thimbleful of wine. It had taken weeks to manage everything, but now it was going to happen, and it did. The altar was the stump of a great felled tree, and the altar stone was a stone gotten out of the ground. The priest and deacons, and a few who were secretly Christians, like Vaslav, sang the lovely hymns of the Liturgy from different parts of the forest. Their voices rose up to God from all around and sounded like the singing of angels among the trees. The guards thought it was the prisoners singing at their work, as they often did.

After Mass a wonderful thing happened to Vaslav. The priest called to him and said, "Vaslav, you know the nuns who are in prison in some huts a mile away?"

"Yes, I know where they are, Father, but they never come out."

"No, Vaslav, they are not allowed to come out, but you must go to them and take them Holy Communion."

"Me, Father?" said Vaslav, amazed. "But I am not a priest; I can't touch our Lord's Body."

"I would be suspected and stopped if I tried to go to the nuns," said the priest, "and so would any grown-up person; but you are a child and a guard's son. You will get in all right. Because it is a time of persecution, you may take the Hosts if I tell you to, just as boys did in the first Christian days in the catacombs."

So the priest wrapped the little pieces of consecrated bread in a white linen cloth, buttoned them under Vaslav's coat just over his heart, and told him to go when the stars were shining.

When Vaslav set out, the giant trees were white with snow, and miles and miles above his head, like fruit on the frozen white branches, hung burning ropes of stars. He crossed his hands over his breast and kept whispering, "Sacred Heart of Jesus, I put all my trust in Thee."

It was a wonderful night. His footsteps were silent on the snow, and a stillness and whiteness and silence were in his heart. He was not even afraid of being caught. It seemed as if, just behind his downcast eyes, a warm light was burning, so that he could not think about dangers, but could only let the clearness of that light shine upon the stillness inside him.

Andreyev happened to be keeping guard that night, tramping up and down to stay warm, turning first one way, then another, and keeping a sharp lookout for prisoners trying to escape. All of a sudden, he saw a little shadow falling on the snow, a shadow that was moving between the long, still shadows of the trees. He stiffened and felt for his revolver.

Then he saw Vaslav coming along with folded hands and downcast eyes. He started at this sight, as if he was afraid, for this was not the way a boy walked unless he was praying! And yes, sure enough, Vaslav's lips were moving.

Andreyev felt furious. The hair on the back of his neck stood up like a cat's hair when it is angry, and he got ready to pounce on the boy. Then suddenly he saw, to his astonishment, that there was another child with Vaslav, a very tiny boy with a little face as bright as the snow in the starlight. Vaslav was carrying him in his arms!

Andreyev wondered if he was dreaming. He had never seen this little boy before, and he wondered, too, why Vaslav carried him, until he saw that the child's feet were naked and bleeding.

Andreyev, who was so kind, forgot all about who the strange little boy could be, or why Vaslav was out with him in the night. He came up to them and stopped them gently. "Vaslav," he said, "this little boy is too heavy for you, and why has he no boots?"

"He is poor," said Vaslav.

"Why are His feet bleeding?"

"For love," said Vaslav.

"But is He a prisoner?"

"Yes," said Vaslav.

"I will carry Him for you," said Andreyev.

"Oh! No, no!" Vaslav cried out. "No one must take Him from me until I give Him to the nuns."

"Yes," said Andreyev thoughtfully, "although they are Christians, they would bathe His feet and warm Him and feed Him. Yes, I feel sure they would love Him as He should be loved." And with that he picked up Vaslav himself and carried both the children in his strong arms to the nuns.

The next time there was Mass in the forest, Andreyev was one of those who sang among the trees, for he, too, had become a Christian; why, no one ever knew, not even Andreyev.

Franz the Server

Tomorrow was the day of the fair. Tonight Franz stood in the orchard, dreaming of the joys of it. All his life, for as long as he could remember, he had longed for the time when he would be old enough to go to the fair with his brothers, and now the time had come.

Franz pictured it all to himself as Hans and Otto had described it time and again: the noise of it, made up of the band, the hum and jingle of the merry-go-round, the chatter of the people, the students singing. He seemed almost to smell it: the smell of sugared apples, sticks of vanilla, camphor on the seldom-used festival coats, the warm candle grease, the scent on the ladies' gowns, all mingled together with the smell of the clover fields nearby, and the clean, hot fragrance of the German summer. Then he saw it: the swaying of lights, the great colored bunches of ribbons and balloons, the painted cars and horses of the merry-go-round, the bright stalls, the mountains of gingerbread and sugared cake, the piles of oranges, the flashing of the fairy lanterns, the surging, laughing crowd of merrymakers!

Franz had worked; he had helped Mother to milk the cows, carried in the sheaves for Hans until his arms ached, and gathered the fruit in heavy basketfuls for Otto. And now he had his own earned money to spend at the fair. The joy of it!

Upstairs on the bed his suit was laid out, the red suit with brass buttons that he wore only for Christmas and great days, and new white stockings that Mother had knitted for him last winter. Even now Hans and Otto were grooming the pony and polishing the brass on the trap. They were starting at sunrise, for it was an hour's drive

and too much in the heat of the day for the old pony; besides, they must have a long day at the fair! Franz jingled his money in his pocket. He threw back his head and breathed great waves of the good clean night. He was no baby; he was nine years old and a wage earner, and tomorrow he was going to the fair.

"O tomorrow, do come!" he cried to the apple trees. And through the darkness, ringing very clear, as sounds do by night, came the clatter of horses' hoofs, over the road, up the drive to the farmhouse, and stopped at the door. Then came Father's big voice like a trumpet down orchard: "Franz, come in. The good priest has ridden over to speak with you."

In the farm kitchen, Franz saw Father and the priest through the open door. They sat each on one side of the settle, drinking their mugs of beer in the firelight. The dew was all bright on the priest's cloak, and his pale face was like brass in the glow of the flames. Franz stood in the door, his heart beating furiously. He knew what the priest's visit meant.

"Franz," said Father, "you are to ride back with the priest. His boy has fallen ill, and there is no one to serve his Mass tomorrow."

It was not wise to argue with Father, but . . . tomorrow! Franz spoke in a very small voice: "I am going to the fair tomorrow."

"What! After the Father has ridden five miles over the road to take you back! No, no, Franz, you get your cloak, and make ready to be off."

Franz looked imploringly at the priest. He was very young; he hardly looked older than Otto, and he smiled at Franz and drew him to his knee. Then he turned to Father.

"No, he shall not come," he said. "I will manage without him."

He lifted Franz onto his knee, and Franz saw how tired his face was, close up. He thought the priest must have wanted him to come very much, to have ridden so far in the dark when he was so tired.

Franz felt miserable. Somehow a shadow had fallen on the fair. He never liked serving Mass, and just now he did not like the priest. He made a little movement with his body to show him that he did not like him, and he hoped that Father did not notice it. But the priest did not seem to notice it himself; he only closed his big hand over Franz's little one and smiled at him. Franz wished that Hans or Otto could serve Mass, but he had been taught this year at the same time that the priest had prepared him for his First

Communion, and the others had never been taught at all.

Franz remembered, as he sat there trying to fidget in such a way as to show his resentment, that he had once told this priest he would like to be a martyr. Now he felt sure the priest was remembering that, too, and it made him feel more uncomfortable and more miserable than ever. "I can't come," he said, "I just *can't*. I *must* go to the fair. You don't understand how much I want to go to the fair!"

The priest answered softly; he really was not at all angry. "Yes, Franz, I do understand. Once I, too, was looking forward to a great fair. There was going to be every sort of good thing there, and it was going to last for what seemed to me a very long time — all my life."

Franz opened his blue eyes wide. "Forever?"

"No, really for a very short time, just my time on earth, my one day."

He went on answering the questions that Franz had thought, but had not asked. "No, I did not go to my fair. I had another invitation, to go to the great Feast the King had prepared, and I answered that invitation."

Franz knew that the King was our Lord, and now He was inviting him to come to His Feast. He bit his lips not to cry in front of Father and the priest. He felt very, very unhappy. "It is funny of our Lord to send His invitations on the days of the fair," he said huskily.

The priest held his hand more tightly. "It is a very big sign of His love," he said.

"I *can't,*" said Franz.

"Very well, He wouldn't want you to come unhappily. Neither do I."

When he had finished his mug of beer and pulled his cloak around him, the priest bade them good night and mounted his horse. He had said no more about the server for his Mass, and for a moment Franz felt the weight lifted from his heart. And then, suddenly, he ran down the road and caught up with the horseman. He looked up at him in the darkness.

"I want to come," Franz said.

After his long ride through the night air, Franz slept deeply. Just before sunrise, the priest lifted him out of bed, still half asleep, and told him to get dressed. He wondered for a moment why he had a dreadful feeling, as if there were a lot of strings tangled around his heart. Then, as he looked out over the fields and saw the little red clouds riding up the sky and the dew golden on the grass, he remembered. Just now Hans and Otto were putting the pony into the trap, or perhaps they had already started.

Heavy-hearted, he followed the priest to the sacristy. He lit the candles sadly; how pale and faint their tiny flames looked. Franz thought of the great swinging lamps at the fair.

The two stood at the foot of the altar. "In the name of the Father and of the Son and of the Holy Spirit," said the priest. "I will go unto the altar of God."

"To God, who giveth joy to my youth," said Franz miserably.

The priest was saying the *Confiteor*. "They are nearly there," said Franz inside. "Through my most grievous fault," he said with his lips.

How long the Mass took! Why, the priest was still asking forgiveness. What a lot of forgiveness it needed to go up to the altar of God! "I wonder if Hans and Otto are riding the merry-go-round now," said Franz inside.

"The Lord be with you," said the priest.

Suddenly Franz hoped the Lord would really be with him, for he was dreadfully afraid a tear was coming out of his eye. "I am not crying," he said inside. "And with thy spirit," said the voice of Franz.

They went up to the altar of God. Franz felt in his pocket for a handkerchief and found none. "Lord have mercy," said the priest. "I never cry," said Franz inside. "Christ have mercy," said a thin little voice, which must have been his.

The Mass went on, and through the server's head, the thought of everything at the fair went on in a woeful procession. He wondered if he would have won a coconut. Would there be donkey rides? He had meant to buy Mother a bunch of ribbons. Perhaps there would be a hundred stalls, and dogs dressed up like brides! The priest had finished the Gospel. "Praise be to thee, O Christ," said Franz, and his voice could hardly be heard at all.

Then Franz shook himself and stared hard at the altar. The priest was lifting the paten with the little Host on it. Franz remembered that he should offer himself with the Host, and for the first time he understood that he *could* do that.

"I came to Your Feast instead of the fair," he said to God. "I didn't want to, but I'm glad I did."

He tried to think of a clearer way to say it, but none came. It came into his mind that there was no one hearing the Mass at all. He wondered if everyone was at the fair. It seemed odd that he, Franz, who longed to be somewhere else, should be the only person at the King's Feast. It would be unkind not to enjoy it. It almost seemed as if it was prepared only for him.

Franz sniffed rather loudly and wished he had a handkerchief; then he squared his shoulders and tried to smile. "I am smiling," he said to God. He was beginning to be really glad he was there; that smile seemed to help. He felt so sorry for the King who had no one but himself at His Feast; it made him forget to be sorry for himself.

"Poor God," he said foolishly, but sweetly, "You mustn't think I would rather be at the fair." He was holding the cruets as he said this to God, and the dreadful tear he had been trying to keep back slipped suddenly down his cheek and fell into the water. The priest seemed not to see it, but Franz saw that tear gleaming and bobbing in the chalice like a diamond in the wine.

As he turned to put the cruets back, he saw something very strange. Just for a moment it seemed as if there was a huge crowd of people in the church, more than he had ever seen. They were all looking at the chalice, which the priest was holding up, and every one of them had a tear shining on his cheek. But what was still more odd was that they were not all German people, but people in all sorts of funny clothes, and some of them were dark-skinned, and some of them wore clothes like in the olden times, and right in front he felt sure he saw his old grandparents, who had been long dead. There, too, were his own mother and father, and many of his friends, and numberless people unknown to him, rich and poor and young and old; but each and every one of them had a tear on his cheek, and an odd little smile on his mouth.

Franz turned back to the altar. The golden cup, in which he knew his tear still shone like a diamond, was covered now. As he looked at it, he felt as if a flock of birds had broken into song in his heart, and they seemed to be singing the words that the priest was now saying: "Come, Thou who makest holy, almighty and everlasting God, and bless this sacrifice, which is prepared for the glory of Thy holy name."

"Come!" echoed the heart of Franz. "Come!" sang the birds in his heart.

He lifted a radiant face, and he knew that a great multitude lifted their hearts with his. For he, Franz the server, lifted not only his soul to God, but also the Heart of Christ, the hearts of all the faithful (for Christ lives in them all). The poor server, who had not wanted to come to the Feast and yet had come, had brought the world with him.

When the priest turned around and said, "Pray, brethren," Franz spoke in a clear, strong voice for all the world, "May the Lord receive the sacrifice at thy hands." And when the priest lifted the chalice in his hands and whispered the words of consecration, Franz saw the tear, which he knew now to be all the sacrifice and sorrow of all the world, turn red and disappear, and he knew that it was no more a boy's tear spilt into the water, but the Precious Blood of our Lord.

That day our Lord gave Franz his second invitation to His Feast. And he received it this time, not with tears, but with joy. So, although he had many years to wait, he went eagerly when the time came at last, from the fair of life to the Feast of God. And offering himself to the God who gave joy to his youth, he offered in his sacrifice, not his one heart alone, but those of all the people who chose to go to the fair.

Biographical Note:

Caryll Houselander

Frances Caryll Houselander was born in Bath, England, in 1901. Caryll, as she is known, and her sister were baptized into the Catholic Church in 1907. Her parents separated when she was nine years old. She was then sent to convent schools until she was sixteen.

Personal troubles caused her to leave the Catholic Church for a while. During these years, she went to St. John's Wood Art School in London. She worked at many jobs and tried other religions.

In her twenties, she returned to the Catholic Church. She worked for the Church as a painter and woodcarver.

Caryll Houselander wrote articles and drew pictures for the *Children's Messenger.* She also wrote articles for *The Grail Magazine*. Some of these were printed in her first book, *This War Is the Passion*, which was published in 1941, during World War II. She also drew the illustrations for the children's book *My Path to Heaven*, written by Geoffrey Bliss.

Houselander wrote many books in her lifetime. *A Rocking-Horse Catholic* tells the story of her childhood and youth. Many have read her book *The Reed of God*, which is about the Virgin Mary.

Caryll Houselander saw the image of Jesus in all men, women, and children. She served the Catholic Church with joy. Her writings have helped many Christians to love Jesus more and become more like Him. She died in 1954.